C000141063

The Sky Village

A Plot In Paradise

Paulo J. Santos © 2021

The Sky Village Assignment

The Sky Village Assignment

Chapter one

September 1991. The beams of daylight reached the grounds of an island in the middle of the Atlantic ocean where a boy lived holding his dream to his heart. He aimed high. The kid seemed to have a certain conviction of which he wandered daydreaming what might he become. Although, he could sense a shadow next to it. A questionable and mysterious feeling he could not quite grasp. Unable to understand this dark cloud next to his big dream he attempted to ignore it. Eventually, he grew and things slowly changed. There, where life pace was tremendously calming and rarely had new exciting challenges to face. Almost like time itself did not exist. The course of his life may or may not have turned the way he planned.

One's fate at the mercy of their will. Not everything in life is as smooth and simple as
it appeared to be. No one had control over this. That's the way it is, life, never quite the way
one choses it to be. All there was to it was that generally, he was a happy and healthy boy who started to view his spectrum with a clear

understanding of what things really appeared to be. He had a lot to learn in his age, mind and heart. There was no total recognition of high quality of validity in whatever he did, for the exception of football skills, but he had merits and consolation at home. To him it was extremely valuable at his tender age.

In the history of mankind no one owned such power in determining the path of their life as
an absolute affirmation of positivity. Certainly, as a young person he thought that was possible

in creating the perfect life scenario. There were some people, however, who had a deeper sense of reality. People who were able to see beyond what seemed real, and had a gift of sensing the channel of communication to a level of wordless feelings. Almost like the surrounding realms of paranormal activity.

Or as if reading someone's aura. A feeling which was like a stamp intrinsically that denoted one's state of being. Noah had that very strong intuition. But what did reality mean to him? He was just a young man who had an aspiring appetite in becoming a professional footballer. One could only dream freely and blissfully, without any doubt or worry. The youngster faced the change of times as it was revealed the unfolding of events that life brought in. Eventually he grew older and shaped his own personality and perspective on life.

His name was Noah. Noah was a twenty seven

year old man who was crossing a difficult stage of his life. It was the transition from the old life to the new one. A new beginning. His unlined face declared a sign of calmness marked by solitude yet the taste of total independence guided by a slightly pointed nose holding the space which separates his dark round eyes to a precise measure of pensive gaze. A singular furrowed line lies mildly on brow to suit the periphery of his oval-like physiognomy. He was not tall nor short. One could say he was an average type, with a somewhat athletic aspect on his stature. Noah had dark skin, tanned by the long hot summer days. His hair was straight, short and black; it looked strong at the root. It's not much of a hair style, today it's somewhat different to yesterday's appearance. It was his way of

being stylish as it was the sort of action he does when he wakes up by combing his hair with his fingers sliding through it.

Noah lived in London then. He moved there three months earlier, at the end of the spring of 2006, in search of a change of life, or maybe the start of a new one. He lived the summer months exploring his new surroundings and the city. Adapting himself to the language and the system and generally being a contributor in the economy. It quickly had become Autumn, it was greyish and it was turning colder, however the winter sun was in sight and satisfying to stroll underneath a patchy sky. Noah found a small studio flat in the west London area of Chiswick, a respectable and trendy neighborhood, well located for links to central

London and international airport, to

accommodate himself and his few belongings, which, together with him, carry the sorrowful
memories of his past and a loadsome of unanswered questions too.

Noah was born in the archipelago of Azores, on

an island named Luminosa, the only offspring of a Spanish mother and Portuguese Azorean father. In his early teens he had to spend most of his free time helping his parents in the green fields. They mainly depended on agriculture by which, at the will of the season,
A fertile harvest would be a blessed relief adding to

his fathers earnings as a carpenter, but this was uncertain work which wouldn't last long anyway. Occasionally his father would leave home for a few days on fishing shifts and return his earnings home. Overall a reasonable revenue. Noah had a normal, simple, almost timeless life for a kid who grew up on an island in the middle of the

Atlantic ocean, with few other kids in the village to frolicking around

with and explore not only the surroundings but also his manhood. However there was so much worth revealing about the place, not only for the sea views and green terracing of the landscape but for all the rare geological aspects of the island. There are other values of reference in the island as in fact the whole archipelago, such as its rich biodiversity and the architectural, cultural, ethnographic and a natural heritage of undeniable significance. Despite the size of the islands, they have a wide range of landscapes, forms and structures derived from the diverse types of subaquatic eruption in the span of time. Its dynamics and the subsequent actions of weathering and erosion, also contributes to such diversity. The islands are composed of several sites of natural, educational and touristic interests.

As a child, Noah dreamt of becoming a footballer,

which he did, to a certain extent.

He never missed training sessions and by the time he turned twelve, was asked to join the local junior team and became a regular player in most matches. Noah had skills and a vision of interest in the game. Collectively, his team paraded a trophy by having won at one of the finals. Noa's dream never reached the point of going on to a professional level. It wasn't a decision taken on his part but one of the course of life.

At the end of summer of 1994 Noah's dad had left him and his mother, most belongings and the estate behind like an old newspaper in a rubbish bin, no words spoken, no warnings, simply vanished. He ran off with a woman who had a reputation of being connected to a gang of drug smugglers. Hard to know what really happened and how he got to know this woman. Things just happen and the course of life takes a different direction. Noah was sixteen.

He had by then a certain expression of maturity yet shaded with a cast of confusion.

When Noah turned nineteen, two years after his father had left home, his dream of football was to be cut short by the unforeseen circumstances and mysterious phenomena that life offers. One day, Noah and two friends of his were enjoying a game of running along the dramatic landscape of the northwest part

of the island, where hardly any houses are seen, the locals and tourists find it very picturesque for its abundance of rare species of plants and trees and the spectacle of their shapes and colors. Some species are plants and flowers endemic to the Azores islands, nowhere else are they found. A rare variety of Azorean laurel, bellflower, blueberry, ivy, scotch heather and Azorean heather and dwarf mistletoe can be found there, a remarkable variety of cacti spreading across the slopes, palm trees, as well as steam and smoke rising from

small holes on the
volcanic ground
making it look like curled
gray curtains connecting
with the heavens. The
island itself
is named Luminosa, Noah
was born there,
and it is the second
largest in the Archipelago.
It spans roughly forty
thousand kilometers
squared, which in
comparison would be just

about the size of
Switzerland and peculiarly
resembling a distorted
letter 'Q'. There everything
looked and smelled like
paradise. The gardeners
and farmers worked daily
to make sure the
landscape was looking
perfect, from the
elaborately cut shrubs to
the
hundreds of unique
flowers and trees.

The three friends were running at a slow pace, in a way that looked more like a lazy running, lacking composure and rhythm, on a road where two vehicles could not pass each other unless one of them parked on the side

of it allowing the other to move forward. A van was

approaching from behind at a reckless speed. The young men heard the roar of the engine getting closer as they moved to the roadside, somehow Noah miscalculated his stance as the third in line and let himself fall further back, not expecting that some malicious or drunk driver would lose control on the lane. At a sudden moment he was hit by the van. A hit and run incident. The impact sharply threw Noah past his friends through the air as his body landed a few meters ahead of them. A strong thud echoed before them not having the correct words to blow out of their mouths or take note of the runaway van's plate number, they just stood

there, still, panting in
shock.

One of the friends spoke
to the other as if he had
just seen a ghost,
although strong enough in
deciding to run as fast as
he could to the town
centre and get help, while
the other waited at the
scene, by keeping Noah
company even

if it were just to stare at him, or by saying something ridiculous to help him cheer up.

 -" We'll soon be kicking that ball about on the pitch, right?"
However his friend wasn't sure Noah was understanding any of the words he had just said.

-" Noah, hold on if you can hear me, stay with me. Don't let go." His friend pleaded in a desperate voice while holding his tears.

Noah broke his left arm, right leg, four ribs and luckily, based on the circumstances, no major injury to his head which could have left him in critical condition, or unable to use his senses in accuracy, or even paralised. It took him nearly two years to recover fully. Maria, Noah's mother, was heartbroken by this,

moreover, for not being able to find the hit and run driver nor having assistance from her run away husband. By then, she was genuinely angry that everything fell on her with such a weight that it felt the world was resting on her shoulders. Maria needed solutions to this problem. She needed to act rapidly to ease the agony of misfortune in her life. Her priority was firstly and foremost to help her son with whatever was at her disposal. Her decision arose during a crisis of tears while in the darker side of her room all by herself.

Noah's mother had decided to sell all the estate to generate an income and live free of the problems by having to employ people to work the land or having to do it herself. She was not strong enough to carry out such tasks daily. The house and land was worth a lot of money, enough to buy a secluded villa in the southwest area of Portugal, pay for her

medication related to diabetes and still have plenty left to add on her will. At this point Noah started drinking. After his father had vanished, being a victim of a hit & run incident, not being able to fulfill his dream and seeing his mother's health steadily deteriorating was all a bit too much to handle. School was a thing of the past. He started pursuing a future not concerning football. But even though he is not sure of what to do next.

Noah was still dreaming, a different sort of dream, one that he could not simply attain by giving his

best effort at it. A type of life that was usually seen on TV or magazine personalities. He knew there would be a long wait in order
to start planning a new life. He had to start somewhere and take action if he wanted to achieve results.

After a long recovery and much thought

and effort invested as to what to do next he

had decided to move to London. England was suitable for him as he loved the language. He had excellent results in his English exams.

However in real life it was more challenging than school learning. Whatever he had learnt he would have the chance to put to use and improve it by practice once settled in the English community. He searched for work and accepted the first job he was offered. His first job as an adult. The very first pathway to his independence by the choice of his decision making.

Noah worked as a waiter in a french

restaurant named "Soleil Rouge", which sounded more like a tribute to Japan, located in the vicinity of London's prestigious Mayfair area, where many celebrities could be spotted splashing out their high earnings with great satisfaction and style. As It was Noah's first job there, he had been on a learning journey,

memorising menus and wine lists, how to hold and carry plates of colourful and well presented food and also present himself by providing a good service to customers. He had never done
this sort of job in his life. He gained knowledge on how to handle bottles and pour of wine, holding glasses, terrines,

positioning of cutlery on setting up the tables, how to speak to customers when taking an order and learning how to use his memory by jotting down on the order pad who had chosen what. So Noah would make references based on a piece of clothing, or its color, or a jewellery item, even drawing a table, numbered to help him deliver the right item to the right customer. It was a new challenge for him. He knew he had not dreamed of doing such a job, however he saw the joy of its intricacies and most importantly it got him a steady and reasonable income. In spite of having a certain negative approach to his job, he usually left home for work in a

generally content mood
and in keeping a good
spiritual attitude, even
though he felt as he could
read the stages of the day,
hour by hour, just by
thinking in advance what
his manager
might argue about as the
day unfolded. Now
he had fallen into a routine
already with some
understanding of his

tasks. Winter passed by while he engaged with his new skills. His life carried on. He maintained a regular phone update of his new life in a different country to his mum to give her reassurance he was coping well and similarly give her peace of mind.

Noah lived in a converted studio flat on the top floor of a Victorian

house, overlooking a
green park big enough to
accommodate a
small row of houses; five,
six at most, one single
whitebeam tree in the
middle of it. It
was a simple looking
green space to stare at
with its borders assorted
by common roses,

abelias, daffodils, thyme
and rosemary shrubs and

common laurel bushes. At the end of the park there was a railway line with a faint sound signal, heard from his studio, every time a train would pass by.

Noah usually left home at around 7:30am for the early shift. That morning was no exception. It was a cool Tuesday morning, late April, patches of small dark clouds hanging in the sky. There was a small presence of sunlight. Trees and shrubs sprouted their buds as a reminder that spring had arrived. He could smell the fresh fragrance of a changing season flying around the city. Noah zipped his jacket up as he adjusted his body to it while walking towards the bus stop greeting some older neighbors, who seemed eager to be noticed early in the morning with the usual "good morning" and " have a good day" comments. He wished the street were empty so there

wouldn't be the need for forcing out a smile so early in the morning, as if to cover up whatever he was still reliving in accordance with the fragmented moments of the previous night all cocooned in his memory lane as if it needed being corrected or understood. He meant no

bad feelings for the old people who he respected, it was more the case in avoiding showing a less pleasant side of him. He simply preferred to hold his half a sleep state of mind to himself. So he got his headphones, hit the playlist on his mobile phone and started by playing a tune, entitled "Grin" by Coroner, a Swiss Heavy Metal band. And so it started another journey to work, just a different day.

Noah also enjoyed quiet mornings in his eccentricity in search of finding scattered visions of

the previous night out,
perhaps
there were answers
hidden there, perhaps
there was nothing much to
recall, but it was

still necessary to gather
an image in order to put
his thoughts in place for
the rest of the day. No
matter the importance of
this.

Gradually he had become a regular drinker although he would not consider himself dependable on alcohol. He was aware it was becoming a constant habit. Surely, he needed to unwind after a long day running around serving tables in a busy restaurant. Moreover he needed to delete all the words his manager used during shift. That thought of deja vu. However, not any drink would he decide to engulf, that was not a matter of being able to afford the expensive wine or liquor, it required a settlement of taste buds which would allocate the suitability of his being, his palate in such a way to be considered the haven of a particular moment calling for a particular spirit. Noah rarely drank ales nor did he have a tendency or urge to purchase a bottle of vodka, gin or absinth. Although he did not binge drink he

didn't buy what he does not enjoy, to put it mildly and plain.

Jean-Luc was the restaurant general manager who was very strict in terms of assiduity;

arrival at work, quality of service, presentation and behaviour towards and in front of customers; an elite of highly recognisable personalities and celebrities seen on tv and magazines. Jean-Luc had a strange manner of eye communication, very expressive. Often, he seemed to carry a message in his eyes overflowing across the

restaurant floor, mostly a display of a message of unpleasant and vague words, which probably wouldn't matter to long-timers, they were accustomed
to this sort of vague, arrogant behaviour, but this was an apparent worry for Noah who was not used to this sort ethical behavioural code. Jean-Luc's conduct had,

seemingly, never bothered any customer, if it were ever noticed.

Noah had gained a special skill in reading the message floating on Jean-Luc's eyes, that was resembling how he used to understand his father, sometimes words weren't needed to know what his father meant to say. Noah analysed the engraved lines on Jean-luc's face, an intense, taunt and uncaring look, mostly, building an image of how his manager would deliver his sermon at the end of the shift. Frankly, it had been a habit that the Frenchman developed over the years, not intentionally but by having committed himself to the job fully and having fallen into a repetitive routine of his life.

Most of the floor staff at "Soleil Rouge" rather humbly ignored the manager more than to be offended by him, which would have become the usual sordid monologue. That's how it was seen by most long-timers, however this tantrum was noticeable and taken as a shock by the new-comers. Noah was crossing the period of

transition from the beginner stage to establishing himself as a full time worker for the firm with a contract in hand. He had grown up to it and showed capacity and consistency over the trial period. While running around tables,

what looked more like a dance with no particular rhythm and pace, a bit like combining
an improvisation of jazz, heavy-metal and classical genres all into one short composition, Noah got the unusual thought that had been crossing his mind lately. He knew he needed a life changing event, another chapter in his life. He knew something was

constantly changing somewhere in the world, even beyond it, something he could not explain by the use of words, however he showed an apparent adaptation to accept this change in himself. It was then a question of whether he would be deeply involved in exploring it or not, a matter of curiosity that sat on his mind which he would observe minutely. How else would he think of

having a feeling without a vision of something yet to occur? Strangely it felt like a premonition.

 "I don't fully understand these thoughts of sudden changes popping up. What is possibly going on around me that stops me from seeing it? Am I going mad?" Noah questioned himself.

"I wonder?" He continued in his thoughts while still performing an improvised dance pattern all along the restaurant floor.

Olga, a Russian waitress, who looks very bubbly in her own posture with her shiny blonde hair, she looked thirty years old, or slightly younger, would pat Noah's back as if to support him in carrying his thoughts through and himself physically. She'd once said to Noah

- "don't let his words reach your heart, hear

the words but shield your heart from them, Jean-Luc has been working here for nearly thirty years, he knows this place better than the owner does, in a way he acts as such, but don't let it get you down". Noah would shrug his shoulders almost in agreement, sympathising along with a short smile, which in a way meant a simple "thanks" without the need of saying it.

-"You will see, a few more weeks to come you won't even think about it." Olga added.

"What did she mean by that?" Noah was puzzled. "Does she have a crush on me or is it something else beyond the honeytrap look on her blue sky colored eyes. Better not get carried away with it." All the while the buzzing atmosphere of chatter, laughter, and cutlery hitting plates, were

sounding throughout the restaurant. Another day was coming to an end. No major events had happened in Noah's life.

The Sky Village Assignment

The Sky Village Assignment

The Sky Village Assignment

Chapter Two

It's 7.30am, Victor leaves home. It was a cool Tuesday morning, late April. Victor approached his silver Mercedes, opened its door, he sat down and his mobile phone rang. On the other end of the line there was another man's voice,

-"change of plans…" the man confirmed.

-" meet me in my office at 11.00am. I've a business meeting before that, do what you want until then." He ordered.

-"Understood, I'll see you later". Victor replied

in an obedient manner. He ignited the vehicle and set off, slowly becoming a blurred object in motion.

It was 10.50am, Victor parked the car outside the office building and made his way
up to the office by the stairway, arriving just on time as he had confirmed earlier on the phone. While taking his step up the stairs he emphasised an expression that something else was on his

mind, maybe wondering
why the plan earlier had
been cancelled at last
minute by someone, who
sounded like higher in
rank
in line to this sort of "dirty
work", or maybe might just
be the sort of posture, in
an act, like
a change of personality,
just before meeting
this man in the office.
Could it be a source who

hinted things could have gone wrong? Could it be that more bloodshed would take place for wasting that man's time? All this was crossing his mind while going up the staircase, to the

second floor. He entered the office greeting the man who was standing shoulder by the vertical ledge of the window's frame, looking casually outside. A hefty person, short blond hair, well trimmed, good composure. He dressed in a black suit and shirt, hard to tell the brand, however it didn't look so cheap. Both hands in pockets he turned to greet Victor, who just stood there, waiting to be informed, either plan 'B' or whatever else next, adding few more words he looked calmly into Victor's eyes,

-" We will wait four more days to make the deal. There's no plan 'B'. We'll wait. It will be held at a different location and time, as soon
as I come to know that information, it will be passed on to you, ok?"

-"Ok, in the meantime what other deals have you got lined up?" Victor questioned the man

mildly, as not to sound disrespectful.This man looked like he meant real business, better not piss him off by being an arrogant asshole.

-" Little is going on at the moment, as you have noticed. As you also know, I'm getting some more contacts. It's only a matter of time before you get the chance." The Man replied bit by bit stretching out his right arm.

 -" If there's anything I can do for you now it's your chance." Victor responded he did not need anything.

Few days later, Noah finished his shift at 18.00. He was invited to go out for a light meal and drinks somewhere else in a different spot of the city centre. The invitation was made by a part-time work colleague, Alberto, who was

a Spanish national.
Alberto and Olga had the
idea to invite him. They
wanted to get to know
Noah a bit more outside
the work environment
as they were intrigued by
his diction and behaviour,
somewhat unusual for
modern

times from a guy of his age. They had a courtship going on between them for about
one year by then, which wasn't noticeable at "Soleil Rouge", the young couple preferred to keep it private. Nonetheless, Noah accepted the invitation and they set out to go.

At the restaurant, they sat at the given table getting acquainted with the place while browsing the menu. They chatted away, finding out a bit more of one another's background. It had been a pleasant time, enjoying their meal and wine and getting further away in the conversation. Nearly three hours passed while they

talked and enjoyed their
time out. They

paid the bill and left happy
with the service and food,
knowing it really didn't
match the
standards of fine dining at
"Soleil rouge", but that
didn't bother any of them.
They headed to
a bar nearby for another
drink before parting ways

to their homes. After having enjoyed their meals and drinks and while walking to the nearest underground station, Alberto asked,

-"Noah, any plans for the near future? Or maybe something sorted out like family, house, car, you know, the usual stuff?"

Noah answered almost without thinking, a bit of a surprised expression was all over his face, clearly not having expected this sort of question,

-" uh I can't figure out what to do, which makes me conclude that maybe there is no such thing for me to think about. No wife, no kids, nothing is really taking hold of me." Noah's mind was still stationary on two words Alberto mentioned- "near future".

-"Sorry for asking. I hope you didn't take it the wrong way." Alberto softened his voice apologetically.

-"That's fine, it's not an insult by asking." Noah answered in a tone that defined accepting the apology. But he continued,

-"Alll know is that I don't want to live this dull and repetitive life as it has been since I started working at the restaurant. Although, as it stands I can resume my life in three words; it goes on."

Olga remained silent, walking alongside Alberto holding his left arm, as the two men talked. Alberto continued,

-"How come? If you know you can't live a life like the one you are living, as you said, then your future is more likely to turn out to be the one you expect,

should you carry on like this,
that is. All it takes is the little time to make a decision, to allow the change to take its course. Are you following my line of thought?"

Noah simply replied "yes". But he knew he was struck by this remarkable comment Alberto made, which sunk down slowly, heavy as a ship's anchor.

-"I'll figure something out." Noa added. " Things happen for a reason, before I find out what the reason is, something must take place from beginning to end."

-"Are you expecting something major to

happen to you?" Alberto questioned curiously.

-"You will probably laugh at what I'm about to say, but yes. I can't tell what it is nor whether it will affect me directly or others, nor can I say when it will happen, nor how it will happen.

Anyhow, this is a feeling that feels real and I

presume it will have something to do with me." Noah explained showing a slight sign of embarrassment for divulging this thought that had been glued to his brain.

-"It's a bit like a premonition." He added.

-"Maybe that's how things are meant to be, how you

are meant to be. Whatever will happen will happen, regardless of what you do right now." Alberto exclaimed.

-"Maybe." Noah responded simply yet in a mystifying way, as if he should continue exploring this subject. That was left at that.

They said their goodbyes, informally, but politely, knowing that the next day they would meet again at work.

At Alberto's place, Olga had just finished showering, while Alberto flicked through pages of a magazine, not paying much attention to it, just looking randomly, like a fainted mirage in the distance, the type of behaviour that one does while something else is in mind. Olga sits at the edge of one side of the bed which is closer to the window and plugs her hair-dryer, switches it on and starts drying her hair combing it with her right hand at the pace of a stroke of affection from one lover to another, as the left hand gently sways the appliance to blow a pattern of wavy hot air. She looks at Alberto and somewhat hesitantly, asks him as softly as she strokes her hair,

-"You are not thinking of asking him, are you?"

-" I'm starting to believe he could fit in. You heard

what he said. He doesn't
have a vision,
a plan for achieving
anything in the future, if
he will be lucky to get
one." Alberto sounded
as if it didn't mean
anything wrong by saying
it bluntly.

-" I will wait a bit longer, in
the meantime, I'll
try finding out a solution to
get us started on

the next task, then I will take him to Victor."

As he spelt out this sentence he approached Olga who gazed at him with a massive question mark in her eyes, sat next to her and started kissing her neck. She giggles in acceptance of his act, drops the hair-dryer, his left hand placed at Olga's left breast palpitating it and rubbing her nipple, but in a way that he is almost pushing the whole of her upper body to lay down. They kissed intensely and continued

displaying each other on a journey of sexual desire and fantasies throughout the night.

One morning in mid June Noah stepped out of the flat. He stopped and admired the sun's bright light, it surely was a beautiful morning. He lit up a cigarette before stepping down the very few stairs. He headed to the nearest coffee shop and took a cappuccino on the go. In the still of the moment he had forgotten about time and space, only the realisation of existence.

For a moment everything around him seemed to have stopped.

Later the same day…

It was about 20.45 hours. Noah was drinking yet another glass of Cabernet Sauvignon, having drunk two glasses earlier while eating

a light meal. He stared at the only painting hung on the wall effortlessly, however his thoughts were all melting into a pool of mental chaos. Looking at the painting was just the channel for mind traveling, in this case the wine has made its cause too. All of a sudden and strangely he stood up and gave the room a good clean. It took him an hour to organise the whole mess. It felt much better. He felt better with himself, at least for a short while. However, having agreed to enter Alberto's circle, the thought of his assignment is persistent. It had become real. Nerves and fear slowly sank down. As a new recruit he will be a part of it.

He was not entirely sure how to act in this role. Nevertheless he would participate and it was that thought of not knowing what to expect which tormented his mind.

Daniel was appointed by Victor to spend
time with Noah on a quiet farm on the southern outskirts of London, where he was meant to show Noah a variety of unseen material like hand guns, shotguns, rifles, ammunition, and diverse amounts of narcotics. He had also
been instructed to teach Noah how to understand

and make use of firearms and become more familiar with the whole process of getting involved in a wiser world. The training of the new recruit was fast paced as any free time available would be spent driving down to the farm and practice shooting at things. Occasionally Alberto and Olga joined Daniel and

Noah to break down the
intensity
of the training and brought
a lighter atmosphere into
having fun on the peaceful
landscape around.

Three weeks passed by
within the ordinary manner
which had long been
lingered around,

like a shadow company, a
presence of something

that is seen moving by but it's untouchable. Noah has developed a deeper friendship with Alberto and Olga who in turn had arranged to get a female friend of theirs
to go out with the three of them whenever the occasion would arise. That was the least of
the problems. One night after work they arranged

to meet Elisa nearby the
restaurant
so they would be able to
explore the net being
thrown at Noah's heart.
Elisa wears a light
smile on the curves of her
thick reddened lips
exposing her white skin.
From the small protrusive
chin to her chestnut
colored eyes forms a
perfect V shape,
dominated by a visible

angled circumflex eye brows in deep darkened abundance. Her broad tip nose is relatively cute, it does not outshine the roundness of her face. Elisa glances at a pile of white sheets spread out unevenly on one corner of a small wooden table. Elisa attempted to pick one out and read it, she couldn't be sure how Noah would react to it. She decided to allow him in, noticing that she might have been curious to read one or two. He realised she had looked, quite intentionally, at that unorganised table with loads of papers stacked on the corner as if to ask him without spilling out any sound. By quickly reading her body language Noah spoke;

-"This is why I write, because I am not so good at talking. I do not consider myself anti-social but on the other hand I am not an easy going type either. This is who I am. Life is really simple, but we insist on making things complicated, as denoted by some philosopher,

I believe. I just tend to think a lot generally and go with the flow on a little imaginary boat navigating adrift until, maybe, one day it will touch land, the same as water running down the stream eventually will meet the sea. I just keep on asking myself how I got to this endless

Asea on a tiny floating vessel sailing over and over again."

-"That sounded to me as philosophical as it did logical." She confirmed by giving away signs
behind this comment she was actually asking herself "what are you? not who are you?", obviously not in an offensive way, Noah didn't

answer what came to his mind, instead
he simply replied with a tone of despair over
a soft sigh along the words:

- "I don't know",
like he had just read Elisa's thoughts and ignored what she had just said. The night light gleamed on roof tops under a delicate

moonlight, Elisa approached Noah knowing, apparently, what she wanted, however not knowing exactly what to expect from a guy who seemed rather unusual, smooth yet owning a strong presence of being.

-"I wish I could be able to record all my important and most relevant thoughts and peruse them

one by one in a blissful meadow
of words." Noah confessed with an extent of sorrow.

He was allowing his feelings to confide with this woman regardless of the outcome. It was apparent that she had an interest in his whole being.

-"It's true we don't always make the right decisions although not always we get what we deserve, it's like a pathway that is there and we ought to walk it. Sometimes we get what we deserve, sometimes it's so much worse than that".

Elisa showed that she is capable of having a profound and effective conversation. She had been glad to be there at that very moment.

Two days later Alberto and Noah meet in central London for a coffee. That was a chance for Alberto to give Noah some insight

into making some extra
money meant by Alberto's
standards. Noah was
asked calmly by him
whether he would be
interested in making
extra money besides
working at the restaurant.
Noah just listened to him
and watched him rolling a
joint while both were
seated on a bench in
Hyde Park. Olga wasn't
present. Alberto explained

superficially how things worked, what it took to be a part of it, his role as well as Noah's and depending on job demands how much the reward would possibly be. At first Noah was hesitant, he shook his head in denial, even though knowing his present job prospect wasn't the option he would rather pursue. He was still young to explore life, surely he must have wanted to thrive further.

****

Victor received a call from the man who he had spoken to at the office asking him to be back at the office the following day, but he was advised

he should carry his gun, if possible
more than one. This call left Victor repeating to himself each sentence the man had said. Could it be a bigger deal, one that might involve more people holding their automatic firearms, or any other sort of gun or inevitably a real presence
of danger and the realisation of death? Every

dodgy business brings with it such potential dangers.

Next day there was a really big deal set for Victor and company. Both sides turned up on time at a car park outside a major wholesale

retailer where there are numerous business owners buying their goods

and ferrying them into their cars, which would not cause such suspicion if they were to buy something. That would be a normal action of any buyer. It would be as easy as placing the goods in the boots
of their cars, only then the exchange could take place with minor disguise. It was business time and they

didn't even get inside the massive

warehouse. It looked old, lacking in care at least on the outside, overall the building had

a fearsome appearance by the neglected care over the years. Victor requested in seeing the material agreed upon; thirty kilos of hashish, ten kilos of cocaine and a briefcase enveloping three light fire weapons, the type of Springfield Armory shotguns and a few boxes of ammunition. All this happening in broad daylight. They have adopted a tradition of acting normally as one would at any time. They are just business men. The more suspicious

the action of their behaviour the more

attention to themselves would be focused on.

On the phone, Samy arranged a meeting with Victor to get the merchandise collected at a small marina in Baixo Pico area at 14.00 hours, which was located inside a white fishermans boat named "Santa Fe'." It was an amount of eighty kilos of hashish ready to be handled from Seroza island, which was only small enough to host a few dozen habitants, and located further north in the Atlantic waters, one mile closer to England. Seroza had a formation of a greenish cover half moon shape spreading over most parts of the island, except for the bays of sandy beaches and the locations of the few human settlers. Had it been an independent sovereignty it would look like a massive plot of land covered in natural vegetation, in comparison to people who lived there. Nevertheless, that was a job that

required determination, courage, awareness, and someone who can carry out a task such

as knowing that at any one time things could take a punitive twist and even meet their destiny's foreseeable end. Victor has dealt
with many dangerous situations in his past criminal life, which he had to improvise upon the realisation that it was either make or break. No looking back. Victor decided to call Daniel,

who was his right arm
man. Daniel was going
to take his place and be in
charge and have Noah
with him for the entire
journey. Samy had
arranged that the boat and
captain would shift along
through the atlantic under
the night sky.

Back in London, Noah
will fly abroad on a

mission to accomplish a difficult task. He is in contemplation with god whether this is something he should do. He is ever more

aware of the perils this brings. There is a sense of doubt in his mind. After all, he had never done anything like this in his whole life. He had asked

for a challenge in life and there it was. Was it too late to pull out of it without painful ramifications? Noah sensed a feeling of electric anxiousness running up and down his body. He laid on his bed staring at an empty white ceiling like a blank canvas ready to be filled up with image,
color and pattern. There was a bottle of red wine in

half on the bedsit table with a single small glass empty next to it. It seemed Noah could not finish that bottle on the night, he had got too much going on his mind. Noah needed, conveniently for him, waking up in the morning not feeling hungover or sick. As clear minded as possible. If only he was able to sleep at all. He listened to a distant wail of siren and the small roar of traffic passing outside, coming

through the ajar window. The little raindrops orchestrated a minimalist background sound as it hit the hard ground. He was the only member in the audience of this vast performance. Every now and then he got the encephalic reminder emerging of how things were just a few months back in time, just like Olga had said, whether she meant a sequence of events would take place in his life that would lead to the present time, was an unanswered question, and probably one which would remain as that.

Noah decided to prepare some personal things to take with him in no hurry. He was not preparing for a holiday anyway. He stuffed a few clothing items into a sporty black leather handbag showing little care for these. He was unaware of the importance of this task. He was in self-judgement. He displayed an expression of something bothering him apparent in his

transfixed look at whatever he did at any moment. He took another sip of red wine that he had poured into the glass, leaving the bottle nearly as empty as he was feeling.
"How did I come to this?" He thought to himself while studying the glass

he holds. Simultaneously, he had thoughts of how he had wished for life changing opportunities not so long ago. The old proverb that says, "be careful what you wish for", was biting him back.

The Sky Village Assignment

The Sky Village Assignment

The Sky Village Assignment

Chapter Three

Morning arrived bringing with it a blasting ray of light penetrating Noah 's room window. He was ready to go. He looked around, grabbed the sporty leather handbag, left the room and headed to meet Victor before heading to the airport. Victor explained the situation which was to follow instructions as allocated to Daniel.

They got on board the flight to Azores. Return tickets for both. However the inbound journey had been intended to happen by sailing a boat loaded with a certain cargo. That was the plan ; fly to the islands, wait for the moment of his assignment, get to the boat with the load ready to leave for England and the rest would follow. Except that was no ordinary task to carry out.

    The arrival at Luminosa Island had with it the presence of a reddened light across the sky. Time of landing was about 11.20 am, on tuesday. Soon after lunch they would be on a shorter flying journey from there to Sky Village.

Sky Village can be reached easier by helicopter, or smaller planes even though it is practically the size of a small country and rather large to carry the name 'village'. An area of six hundred kilometres squared. The obvious boat arrivals meet straight ascending, highly breathtaking views yet challenging roads up to each town. A sight of mineral resources and a wealthy display of geology formations. There is also a volcanic mineral pool that is one of the most iconic and famous destinations on the island. An attractive time spent for the few adventurous tourists. An island mostly with small hillsides and almost flat grounds above. It's highest point in land is two hundred metres high. Easy to reach by foot. Population is minimal for its size, there is on average as many as forty five thousand inhabitants. The whole island is

scattered in irregular patterns
of small villages, and towns each one provides a central area with bars and convenience shops, and residential areas. Sky Village is located above an active triple junction between three of the world's large tectonic plates - the North American plate, the Eurasian plate and the

African plate -, a condition of events which has emerged into existence of many faults and fractures in the region. It is defined by a line of subaquatic volcanoes and island mounts that extend far north and south atlantic. These islands are actually some of the most unusual shapes in the world and definitely some of the most beautiful landscapes.

Sky village certainly is the highest point of neighboring islands. But there is a downside to it. Experts suspect Sky Village could crumble down at any time, moreover, it would be much more vulnerable whilst an underwater

quake trembling the
tectonic plates occurred.
The seismic events taking
place here have formed
this massive cuboid island
with its walls jagged,
rugged, ripped, as if a god
were pulling it out of the
ocean bed with an almost
accurate geometrical
shape and sheer power to
leave
its surface is four hundred
meters above sea level.

This island is the final product between nature and god, surely. There is no other island nearby or indeed anywhere else which resembles a geometric rectangular formation

as Sky Village does. The island's volcanism is associated with the rifting along the triple junction plates. The spread of the crust along the existing faults and fractures has produced many of the active volcanic and seismic events, which helped shape Sky village. It just seems

to keep on going toward the heavens, as if by a mind of its own living up to its name.

Everyone there knew how nice it felt to switch off the alarm clock in the morning and go back to sleep. The one negative aspect was that it made people late to school, which wouldn't be too far from populated areas, anyhow, or to their small office, to their business. And the force turned into a bad habit, so bad and big, it made some people lose their money, their career, and their credibility – because punctuality was a sign of being responsible in the rest of the world and life in general terms. That was almost ignored here,

not intentionally but by the norms of living habits. Some people lived happily with the little they had.

Others may have wanted
to achieve
higher standards of living
and acquire loads of
material things, but in
order to attain their goals
they had forgotten to enjoy
life in the present.

    After the arrival the rest
of the day was to have a
couple of drinks, walk
along the almost perfect

flatness of the ground, in particular areas at the island's top and just try to eliminate certain thoughts mostly on Noah's mind. There he felt closer to home which was at a distance of just over one hundred kilometers away. Some positive grounds of reassurance, even a boost to his confidence. The two young men stroll along a quiet street leading to a small crescent where a cozy restaurant was located at the corner of it. Daniel seemed to know where to go and what to do. Yet one more day

left to rest, explore and enjoy the island's marvellous sights and whatever else it offered for amusement.

Tony, who was Noah's cousin, had frequently been involved in little fights, conning amateurs and being conned by those already established in this sort of dirty business, harassed by other people alike who had launched themselves into the world of criminality, at a rather early age. God knows why this had happened while being so young. He got to learn the tricks really quick. Tony spotted Noah and Daniel walking slowly giving signs that they were about to enter a bar. It was a rather hot day. Tony went in the same direction, for what it seemed he was either making sure whether it was his cousin, or in an acting way to get by unnoticed by him. If the need was necessary Tony would approach

without hesitation. Tony does not know Daniel, perhaps the reason for standing back.

As planned the mission was set to be held at 18.00 hours at Sky Village in a remote region which is mostly industrial, two days after the landing,

Thursday, but only when Daniel is meant to walk away from the target.

Early morning on wednesday one day before the big event Noah was walking by himself feeling uncomfortable within. All of a sudden many doubts arose and simultaneously a lot of questions were also

raised. He found himself, then reflecting on the whole situation he got into. He needed to stop. Trying to adjust his thoughts however he was unable to figure out how to get composure, self confidence, determination. Though, confidence was what
he lacked the most at that point. That was his REAL

self being switched on in real time. He

was still unaware of the number of things that could go wrong and the repercussions of it if everything would happen as planned. He looked like in a trance. He had lost sense of time, location, purpose and affairs. He was just stationary, right there. He looked as if he was the one who had been hit by a dose of a powerful narcotic.

There are surely more important things in life than attaining what someone else might see achievable when they may be well capable in achieving it themselves. Just because one does or achieves something it doesn't mean Noah should do the same. Ironically he wanted a life change after moving to London and he got it. Perhaps not in the way he hoped for. Maybe there were little uncertainties that may bring him some sort of reward. A throw at hope. He had decided to accept Alberto's invitation which

eventually mounted up
and led to that point. The
state of euphoria hit him.
By the end of
the following day he would
need to be ready
to take a shot at his target.
How was he going to
overcome the current fit,
assess it and be in control
of it up to then? He was
unable to reach

composure with such ease.

Early afternoon, the pace picked up on both emotional and psychological levels. Noah found himself wanting answers and solutions and less inclined to idle talk as a result. He was looking impatient as his boiling blood ran within, displaying an unusual body agitation. A less common sight on his part. Time was getting closer, in contradiction, he was thinking it was taking forever. As the night sky fell through the island Noah couldn't seem to be able to adjust himself. He bought a bottle of wine and stayed in his room alone in hope the alcohol would help him sleep.

Thursday morning set but there was no sign of Noah who had hardly slept and decided to wander through dawn. Eventually he turned up for lunch. It was early afternoon, the pace picked up on both emotional and psychological levels. He found himself wanting answers and solutions and

less inclined to idle talk as a
result. Time was ticking near the assignment
at the serene Sky Village island.
It was nearly 18.00. It was a bright evening filled with a thin fresh breeze. The streets were calm, hardly any vehicles or people were to be seen. A few tree branches gently dance along to the wind's

mild blowing at the back row of a mechanical site. It had a great view and Noah seemed to be memorising it as he walked

alone into position and assembled his light weapon as he had trained. He lit up a cigarette and waited to the point of seeing Daniel and his target arriving. Noah was shaking and continuously trying to keep hold of his nerves. He checked around analysing all views and whatever else goes by. All he waited for was

the moment Daniel had to walk away from the target so he could accomplish his first assignment. That was the deal made for him

to be accepted in the gang.
Five minutes had passed on.

Noah faced another obstacle that leaves his body semi-paralised, in agonising ecstasy. A tremendous shock to his senses. As soon as he laid eyes on his target, through the reflector sight of the gun, in a matter of a millisecond he recognised that the figure who he was meant to shoot down for the first time in his life was his father, Samy. The man who had long ago left his mother and himself behind, was right there, a shadowed image in a range of forty meters

or so. The man who arranged the cargo of

narcotics being shipped had also entered the same gang as well as another affiliated ring of smugglers, as in fact he had done it for a long while. A middle-man gaining trust from those who have more money and power. Noah had to zoom closer to make sure it was Samy, however he knew well that that person talking with

Daniel was his target. "Dad?" Noah called in silence. Ten seconds seemed an eternity. Noah was stunned and obviously swirling in his own thoughts. Hundred different questions arose in mind in ten seconds, still reeling from his fathers sight in chaotic rationality, Noah relaxed his index finger from the trigger. He could not think straight right then, he took a look at both sides and dropped back his wide open eyes again, to double check whether that was just a mirage or the real thing. Adrenaline rushed intensely over his whole body. He could hardly contain the fast pounding of his heart.

He retrieved the gun, laid it on the ground where he sat next to it, not knowing what to do.

He couldn't kill his own father in his first attempt to kill someone ever. It must be bad enough to turn a gun and pull the trigger at someone, then having to carry the flash-backs depicting it, let alone carry the burden for the rest of

his life for the very first execution being his father. What can he explain to Daniel who
in turn will need to to explain to Victor? Noah was walking on a thin rope between two mountain peaks.

This, however, raised the question to himself, "what might have you done, dad? What might you have done?"

Shortly after...

-"What the hell happened to you, Hey?"
Daniel questioned furiously, as he returned.

-"Do you know the consequences for not

having accomplished your mission? If we do not do this
today, we'll be the prey instead, do you understand? Is that what you want?" Daniel spat out question after question while Noah was pensative of the sight of his dad. Daniel's words were obscured by Noah's thoughts. As he walked a few steps over looking

around to see whether Samy was still there. It all seemed like a terrible dream.

-" It was my dad." Confessed Noah sounding stunned.

-" That was my father who you were talking to. Did you know that? Did you bring me here knowing all along he's my dad?" Noah

got a little agitated,
enough to even puzzle
Daniel.

-" No man, I have met him
twice some time back
while both got involved in
a couple of jobs,
that's all. I had no
knowledge about your
relationship with him."
Daniel responded being
honest about the fact that
he had met Samy in the

past, he continued while Noah waited for the rest of his reply,

-" How long have you spent with me so far? Have you ever witnessed me asking Victor for details? I am told what the situation is and I follow the necessary arrangements. I am quite shocked too, small world." Daniel explained.

-" Sorry Noah, really I am, I didn't know about it. And now what do I do?" Daniel struggled to grasp the understanding of the past twenty minutes.

Both needed to get calmer and figuring out what to do next, and dealing with

such a complex dilemma.
They left the place in
silence
carrying thousands of
distraught thoughts. They
returned to the hotel and
separated from each other
awaiting further notice.
Daniel simply spoke a few
words,

-" I'll be in touch in a little
while."

Noah nodded his head as he retired in his room.

Noah encountered a twist in his path, a lapse of time on a journey to discover a new dream. For instance, he no longer dreamed of achieving football success, he was too old to pursue such a goal. He dreamt of waking up in the morning in a remote place away from the major hassles of everyday life. He realised in a very short time he wasn't born to do such a thing. He tried. Noah got his thoughts in order

he had to find a solution that would spare his father's life, save him from committing a terrible crime act by taking someone's life and find a place where he could not be traced by Victor or "the man" without having to look over his shoulders.

It reached the end of the day and supposedly the last day at Sky Village. Noah had explained himself and convinced Daniel in talking to Samy. Noah wanted answers that would help him in deciding how he would get out of there swiftly and undisturbed. Hiding this fact from Daniel was paramount.

-"Look, I want to find out a couple of things from him before I send him to the other side, personal things." Noah spoke fast and firm.

-"He is probably a bastard
and deserves it for what
he's done to me and my
mother too, but
I have the right to find that
out from my old man.
I am convinced that he
has been a hard bone
to chew from", he
continued steadily,

-"Just give me a couple of hours or so. I need to understand a few things from him."

   Slightly resentful, Daniel held his thoughts while staring deep in Noah's eyes, trying to read any little signs that may lead him to believe Noah was up to something. Luckily, after a few seconds' pause,

Daniel agreed to allow him to meet Samy at heaven's bar. However, Daniel wanted to be in sight of both.

At the same time the thought of Victor crossed his mind.

-"How are you going to explain your visit here with me?" Daniel asked.

-"Like father, like son, right?" declared Noah, which sounded satisfying enough for Daniel's ears.

-"He's just expecting us to ship the cargo, he doesn't know I am here to eliminate him and it will remain that way."

-"As far as we are concerned, I am the new

guy as your partner in crime and happen to be his son, who he hasn't seen for twelve years, coincidence? Maybe, certainly not impossible. This is here and now and it's a fact. The reality of things is that it was a shock for both of us." Noah confessed while sipping a drink of martini rosso.

Noah met Samy, his father, who started to declare apologetically, a type of confession like tone on his voice :

-"Here people see no use of having time. The only reminder of the day's cycle is the sun which acts like a guideline hanging enduring hours above functioning as a calendar of light. The only thing one needs to know is the difference between day and night. Nobody is ever in a hurry to do anything. They don't need to set up their alarms nor be worried they'd miss their appointment, because none of that is relevant here. Everyone can do as they please, whenever they like, there are regulations to obey though, however internally it works with the structure of an offshore administration ." Samy looked to his left, reaching his son's eyes . Noah heard him but decided to go straight into anger mode by asking :

-"Why did you leave us? By the end of 1996, two years after you left, mum sold the land and all the estate, to secure us with some stable
future. We were unable to look after it properly anyway. That happened after the accident I
was a victim of." Noah claimed lowering his face

to the ground.

-"I left because I was naive...and I'm sorry I wasn't there before or after the accident. I had no idea. What kind of a father does that make me?" Samy replied almost soundlessly.

-"I helped raise the estate. I worked hard to keep you in school. I was the only provider. Deep in my silence, I knew I had to do something else. Something new, an adventure somewhere far from there." He continued slowly raising his tone.

- "Only recently I moved here. For the looks

of it, I have this hunch feeling that I must find

another place to settle and probably die alone somewhere else." This sounded to Noah that his father had probably known the reason for his son being here. Noah asked in curiosity,

-"Have you ever regretted leaving us?" He is fixing his eyeballs right up his fathers face.

-"I can't live a life that includes regret in it. You either live or not." This might have sounded as a good excuse to Noah, in any shape or form that was not the case for Samy.

-"I took chances, one after another, which all became the experiences of my life, therefore I don't see it as regret but an irretrievable failure on my part, in some cases." He added.

-"How did you end up here, only as far as one hundred and twenty kilometers away from

mum. Why haven't you ever bothered to show up?" Noah kept on bombarding questions at him.

- " Mum suffered enough distress, you need to set her free, even though you were the one
who ran away. It would be painful one last time for her but at least she deserves being told in her face. You ran off like a coward."

-"I don't need any part of the settlement, if that is your concern."

-"You wouldn't get one bit." strongly affirmed Noah. A large amount of realism seemed to have broken out at the discussion between the two on the subject of family crisis. The core of the problem was that they were victims of their past.

But that led to the unavoidable question Noah feared to be asked.

-"How did you end up down here, son? Daniel isn't the executive type of person. I met him a couple of years ago in Cape Verde. Where have you two met?"

-"We met in London, where I currently live." Noah responded.
-"Right." Said Samy.

Noah asked his father where he lived and a lot more questions too, while in the near but yet inaudible distance stood Daniel waiting impatiently. He had smoked three cigarettes in just under twenty minutes and in that time he checked his wrist watch numerous times. He looked freakishly, short stepping from one side to another.

As it turned out that Samy was there for a short period of time where he was needed in helping a few dodgy jobs being overlooked.

He lived in Cape Verde. Samy had left Maria and Noah a long time ago. Whatever his intentions were, most of them hadn't turned out to be what he expected. He knew he had to try regardless of the outcome. He fell for a girl ten
years younger and she had become his gateway to a more dynamic but

also dramatic life. It wasn't always easy overcoming all hindrances he faced and in the end he ended up alone as she, too, ran away from him. The lover Samy had left him in Cape Verde and flew to Spain.

A couple of years earlier Samy had started having seriously painful headaches, so he had decided to visit the doctor. After weeks of treatment and dealing with this illness as it was still fresh news he was ready to make a change of life. He considered all the possibilities in order to start planning a step by step exit from the gangs circles and simply his way to the

future as well as he could.
When the doctors
discovered a malignant
tumor in Samy's brain,
they told him he only had
roughly twelve months to
live at the most. Two
years have passed and he
was still going, except, at
a much slower pace. He
may live much longer,
or it could happen
tomorrow, no one can tell

for sure. So it may seem plausible that he should live as he pleases. Certainly this lifestyle will have detrimental effects on the healing process. He knew that that was the beginning of the end. Noah just wanted to keep in touch with his father as much as possible. Even if for the purpose of letting him go safe and unharmed. The same wish

applies to Maria, his mother, who had been constantly on his mind during
this hazardous and surreal ordeal. As for Samy, one could say as the popular quote "old dogs don't learn new tricks", he surely was trying.

Still on Thursday night.

Noah was out on his own; he needed space
to figure things out. If there was such a chance. He also needed to give Daniel space to gather a story to inform Victor as that event was surprisingly shocking even for him under the circumstances of the criminal world.
Daniel decides to go out alone for a while. He calls

Victor in London. He reports that there's a problem with the boat's engine.

-"We have a problem, Victor, we have to postpone the job for two days." Daniel informs with uneasiness in his voice.

-" why?" Firmly asked Victor.

-"I was informed that there's a problem with the engine of our boat. It can be fixed by the end of tomorrow. That means the job can be done the day after by the agreed arrangements.

The merchandise has already been placed in the boat." He resumed.

Victor kept silent for a moment. Then he just said:

-"I'll call you back shortly." And he hung up.

Daniel was slightly disturbed and frustrated. "Damn, what if Victor suspects this is all untrue?" He asked himself while lighting up a cigarette. He headed to the hotel where they were staying. On the way he called Noah, who missed the call. Or maybe he didn't want to answer it. Noah is probably trying to figure out how to exit smoothly from this risky situation.

Daniel was getting sick and worried about the whole thing. As he browsed on his mobile phone he received an incoming call. It was Victor.

-" As soon as the engine is fixed, go ahead with the job. Except for the timing of Noah's mission." He said.

-" Ok, I'm listening." Replied Daniel somewhat relieved.

-" Exactly two hours after you get to know that the boat is ready you will have to find a way to get Samy alone. Are we clear?" Victor sounded vehemently. He had a fine substance of speech. Just like the man whom he had spoken to at the office back in London.

-"Certainly." Daniel responded succinctly.

Immediately he called Noah back but there was no answer. Both, in different parts of the town, were having a drink. Each one trying to figure out what was wrong and how to proceed next.

In the meantime, it turned into dawn on Friday. Noah didn't sleep at all. He needed an escape plan to

spare the life of his father and an
opportunity for him to resolve this issue simply by vanishing off the island and retiring from
the gang altogether. Eventually going his own way temporarily. He started having fragmented thoughts of realisation that this sort of life is
less than pleasant and it goes against his purpose

of living according to his principles.

Meanwhile in London the well dressed man in the office reached the phone and contacted an acquaintance in Luminosa Island. The man informed his source that an unforeseen circumstance had arisen and it needed to be resolved. Khalid, the male voice responding, was meant to investigate this matter within hours. The man in the office wanted Samy dead. Khalid was told to look into it and take care of the situation. Khalid was a Moroccan

national, in his fifties, who owned five fishing boats. He's been a fisherman for whole life.

Certainly he has seen enough events over the years in this region of the Atlantic waters.

The man in the office in London was Richard Caldwell, a businessman in his late fifties, who had succeeded having invested in stock shares, property market and fruit imports from Spain and Morocco. He was well established and connected amongst sources alike in either work field. The Moroccan government was still modernising managerial systems and career perspectives for foreign entrepreneurs, while also implanting a number of investment funds into the economic capital and beyond.

Richard's business there turned into reality just a

the right time and being able to sustain it had been very difficult, and often against the will of the government exporting policies, luckily he had met a man named Khalid in Spain where

his business was thriving who had helped in resolving Richard's issues with technical difficulties and language barrier.

Samy had run away with Richard Caldwell's wife, Jenny. She died suddenly after falling off from the fifth floor of a hotel balcony while in Spain on a trip to a friend's birthday party. One hell of a freaking accident one could hardly explain. Samy had not been present at the moment of her death. He had been in Cape Verde due to his medical conditions. Mr. Caldwell strongly believed that Jenny not only had been taken from him, but was also killed by Samy. He wanted Samy dead, regardless how far away he may have been, that was not a considerable matter for Richard.

Noah's affable approach with Elisa had turned mutually strong by then. Distance was just a matter of three days away before seeing

each other again. She will follow, as soon as he's ready.

For Noah there had been a stronger attraction to the

unusual, challenging, controversial ideas and methods of having things resolved. He looked pensively in a maze. He had always been an acute observer and deep thinker, particularly when it was related to emotional or psychological health status. He's been approaching and solving problems that seemed a little too overwhelming or

difficult, on other days with complete confidence right up
to that moment. The desire is to make progress, positive change, and improvements in his life that lead to a more empowered feeling. A purpose of Being. Instead it occurred to him that these people around him dragged

corruption into paradise island.

Statutory rules were nearly absent from this illegal monopoly of practices.

Noah's concern now is to free himself physically from there and also of being able to enjoy life either controlling the amounts of alcohol intake or completely withdrawing himself from it. At his wits end he makes yet another decision to embark on a new path, a new life. Perhaps, out of London and not returning to the Archipelago either. He has chosen to pursue a peaceful lifestyle, living one day at the time. A new place somewhere, another country maybe, but most certainly out of trouble. Only time will tell whether that is

the right bound. Noah called Daniel. He'd mentioned he needed time alone to gather

hold of his thoughts. Daniel understood him, and in a split second suggested meeting him at the bar across the road in the hotel.

They met at the bar. Daniel looked jittery. He seemed very unpleasant within himself. Whereas Noah was in a dopey-like state, gazing at nowhere in particular, the sort of look fading into the distance.

Daniel started talking by pointing out there would be a new time for the job to take place.

-" I called Victor and told him there was a problem with the boat's engine. I just hope he won't check if this is true or not." He said that while still thinking of his very own words.

-" What did he say about the rest of the matter?" Noah asked.

-"I told him the boat should be ready by the end of tomorrow." He paused a bit, then continued:

-"Victor said that two hours after the aforesaid

problem with the engine, you must carry out the job."

-"right. So, what time is it meant to be?" Noah replied not showing much interest.

-"We leave it at the same time it was originally scheduled for." Daniel made sure he sounded like he was still in charge of the mission. His voice changed tone gradually when he turned to Noah;

-" Did you go to see your dad?"

-" No. I've been wandering around. I don't know where he lives. I just needed amending my thoughts. I can't block the situation." Noah said, showing a corner of a forced smile.

-" Look, I understand he's your dad, which leaves me in an awkward situation. Are you sure you can do it?" Daniel questioned somewhat heartily.

-" I'm trying to compose myself and reemerge into

it. I've been thinking about my mother and how she would react if she knew We're both
here after all these years." Noah sounded like he was feeling home-sick.

-" Yes, I get that, man. I leave you alone to figure out whatever it is you need to. But just
so you know, I bear the burden of your

replacement." Confirmed Daniel.

He didn't want to go too deep into the-family-business-thing. And he raised his drink as he got up. He gave two steps as he was leaving.

-" Do you know what he did?" Noah asked, raising his voice louder than usual. Daniel looked back at him and replied firmly:

-" I get to know what to do and not to know
what has led him to do what he did." And he left.

Noah decided to call his girlfriend who had been highly worried and very emotionally involved in all of it. He'd been thinking of her too, perhaps not as much as she would like to, amidst the embroiled and bizarre twist of events. Elisa was waiting for the moment to be with him. She had been living in the expectation that he'd call her to let her know he was ok. That was it. They exchanged a few loving words and Noah decided to give her a hint of what had been happening the last few days.

-" my mission turned out to be a nightmare." Affirmed Noah.

 -" the target was my dad. I recognised him in an instant and I couldn't do it." He continued.

-" what happens now Noah? What about you? When are you coming back?" Elisa asked anxiously as she waited for any reason not to worry about his well being.

-" Here is the plan I have in mind; I will have enough time to help my father escape before the time Daniel is meant to meet him. And the fastest way is by flying out of here. Because the boat isn't at Sky Village but somewhere off." He explained.

-"How about you? How are you going to go unnoticed?" Elisa asked with fear on each word.

-" I'll be fine. I will leave my phone behind as soon

as I know my dad is out of here. So I
won't know who's calling at all. I have something lined up for making my way out." Noah was giving as many details as possible to her.

-" And where do I fit in in all this, Noah?" She questioned.

-"That depends ..." He said with a grin on his face. And continued,

-" I've got all the important contacts I need written down. Will you be ready to meet me anywhere, honey?"

-" What are my other options?" I'll just have to wait and see, won't I?" She replied.

-"I've got to go now. I'll call you soon, babe." Noah gave her some sign of assurance.

Elisa simply answered; -"I miss you."

Noah has been reliving much too frequently the

moment he saw his dad over the last
a couple of days. A thought rushed over his whole self; by whatever means he wouldn't thwart his father. The inimical situation was constantly spinning on his chaotic state of mind. He needed to recompose himself, yet again. All
the little details planning the escape unharmed

were hopping in his head all the time. He just needed putting them together and to act on them. Noah knows he doesn't have much time left.

The Sky Village Assignment

The Sky Village Assignment

The Sky Village Assignment

Chapter Four

The escape :

Samy was lying in bed at a friend's house where he was staying in exchange for his involvement in dealing a few blocks of marijuana into Spain, when his mobile phone rang. It was Noah. At first he was hesitant in answering the call. The thought that he'd be talking to his son was pleasantly felt. Samy never thought he would meet his son after such a long time and under this circumstance. However, he was concerned in being overheard at any details which might have been spoken and unveil unnecessary drama to an already situation in turmoil. Even the thought of phone calls being bugged crossed his mind. Yet he answered the phone in little hesitation.

-"I need to talk to you in person, urgently. Meet

me at the White Rock Park in 30 minutes." Noah sounded almost like giving a command to his old man.

-"What is the problem? You sound like you're being chased, what is bothering you?" Samy asked in a very relaxed manner yet continuously looking around him.

-"Dad, the reason I've come here with Daniel is that.. that I accepted an offer to do a job. A really dirty job. I don't know what I was thinking then. I guess I just wanted to change the way things were." Noah confessed in an unusual rapid speech.

-"Whatever it is, you're here now." Samy tried to assure him.

-"Dad, you shouldn't be alive by now. I didn't know it was meant to be you." Noah added.

-"What are you talking about?"

-"Earlier at around 18.00 you were with Daniel. I was a short distance away from both of you. I was meant to shoot you dead right there, because that's what I came here to do. I recognised you in an instance.

I was unable to do it, so I had to talk Daniel into delaying it". Noah delivered the news.

-"Right!" Exclaimed Samy however not fully surprised.

-"So, I came up with a plan for you and I to escape."

-"...And that is?" Asked Samy in a joking tone.

-"Well, I bought you a ticket out of here. There is a flight tomorrow to Luminosa Island at ten past three in the afternoon which from there you will change to a flight that will take you to Faro. Mum and I bought a nice and secluded villa near there." Noah continued unfolding his treasured plan to his father.

-" Noah, calm down son. What is meant to be will happen. Ok, I'll meet you there! Everything is ok. Just make sure you are safe and relax." Samy

didn't show concern for the situation in his voice
but he can't let his son down, who is risking himself in turn.
The meeting between father and son took
place with a little story that is the reason why Samy ran away all those years back in time.

****

The story with Tony:

Tony, Noah's cousin, was twenty nine years old, skinny, 1.70m of height, oval shaped face features, small curved nose, deep black eyes to match his strong eyebrows, straight long black hair, clean shaven and well tanned. He had an apparent look
of a Rock and Roll person. He was active and he was also very articulate. He was seen with a book under his arm firmly against his body walking like

a rebellion in love. Just a couple of hours earlier

he had sort of spied on Noah and Daniel entering a bar. Why was he hiding? Didn't he want to be seen? Maybe he wasn't too sure if the person he saw was Noah. Perhaps he may have recognised Noah but didn't want to interfere with him and Daniel. As it turned out, nothing he had kept secret was actually detrimental to their relationship. After all they have fallen into the hands of a pernicious fate.

In the middle of the day Tony was walking very calmly alone with a couple of books in his hand, again. His hair was flapping against the wind. As he walked down a narrow residential street he heard a whistling tune and looked towards where the sound was coming from. There was a hand waving. It was Samy on the other side on his way to meet Noah. Tony crossed the street to meet him. They talked for a short while and even exchanged laughter judging the expression on their faces. Just before leaving for his destination, Tony was given a small brownish package which, in turn, placed it together with the books he was carrying.

Noah was crossing an evident downtrodden

struggle in his life, having faced so many events which left him soul searching. In silence and
stealth of an angry grown man. The radio plays faintly in the background. He composes his posture.

Noah knew he would be called by Daniel and meet him at the small hotel bar where he was staying, meant to go and get the new attempt to get the situation resolved. Time was running

out. Noah had come across some medication tablets which he spotted in Samy's car when they met at white Rock park. Medical treatment for Samy's brain tumour.
At first he thought they were headache relief tablets. An occurring idea crossed his foresight.

As expected Daniel called Noah and both met at the hotel bar. When Daniel arrived, Noah was already seated having martini rosso.

Daniel spoke firmly:

-" We need to go."

-" I will finish my drink first. Join me!"
Noah responded straight in his eyes.

While a pause of silence bridged both, Daniel remained standing ordering the same drink as Noah's. Silence took over a minute or two before

an affirmation flew out of
Daniel:

-" You can't do it. I sense you
want to pull out. But
I will have to do it instead.
You can't stop me if you
don't want to be there."

As Noah was digesting these
words staring at his drink
held by the palms of both
hands, Daniel's mobile
phone rang. He answered by
a slight movement of his
body looking outside through

the bar's massive glass window as his martini rosso is left on the bar. At this point Noah instantly reached a small folded paper out of his shirt pocket and dropped it into Daniel's drink. He stirred it with his index. The bar man is wiping the bar and replicating the gesture as if the beverage had just been served

on that very second as Daniel turned back straight,

still standing up and continuously talking on the phone. He sipped down half of it in one gulp. Noah was still in the same position. His thought was that he needed a ten to fifteen minutes wait before the effect took place. He glanced to check the time. He
turned to Daniel in agreement to get going. They
left the place in complete silence and walked towards the car where the weapon

was ready assembled. Daniel unbuttoned his shirt a little while placing his left hand on the driving wheel of an old Ford Escort. Noah pretended he hadn't seen this.

It was a short drive to the mechanical site anyhow, ten minutes at the most. Daniel continued having double visions and rushing heat from chest up to his head while reaching their destined point. As Daniel slows down the car he becomes more incoherent showing an apparent unpronounceable discourse, an attempt arises from Noah by force head crushing Daniel against the steering wheel enough times to leave him out of his senses. The car hits the foot way at an angle to a halt as Noah flees to meet his father who is just at the back of

the building. In a frantic rush they leave the quiet street in

Samy's car heading down to the pier
where they will take the fishing vessel to the next island and from there they fly out.

Khalid was down at the pier observing any suspicious activities in and out of the boat with a supposed technical failure. He was a fisherman, he was working late on the fishing nets of his own boat

which was no apparent
reason to be a valid spy.
There was an obvious
reason why he was
down there at a late time of
the day. The glare of
the sunset was slowly fading.
A car approached the end of
the marina. Father
and son stepped out of the
car calmly yet both looked
behind their shoulders to
confirm whether they had
been followed. Their turning
of heads in

all directions indicated that they were more suspicious than disguising the need to flee the
place altogether. Both walked towards a smaller trawler, compared to all the nearby yachts in the

marina, it looked like they knew where they were heading to. In order to reach the trawler they had
to walk past Khalid's boat. Samy looked at Khalid with a

certain degree of doubt crossing his mind and simultaneously engaging in a fresh talk with Noah for the purpose of being ignored as they moved closer to their fleeting vessel. Once they boarded it, they encountered a man in his early thirties, very dark skin, curly black hair and a strong stature which almost overwhelmed the sizes of father and son, who happily greeted them in and rapidly prepared himself to untie the trawler for the outbound sailing. That man was Tony's friend, Marco, who owns the trawler. He worked in a bank branch of the nearest town and had a great interest in fishing and sea. He had been a close friend of Tony's from school days, back in Luminosa island, where Noah was also from, becoming aware of a certain turn of events that required his aid, even at a cost of a large sum of cash which he refused to accept.

Marco felt the situation needed his asset vessel and was inclined to help his friends even knowing of the potential hazards that it entails.
Khalid saw a chance to fulfill Richard's request.

He got hold of his weapon, without a hint of hesitation he fired two shots aimed at Samy, one of which hit him on his right shoulder and knocked him down. Noah crouched puzzled by the event yet attentive to check on his father who was in pain, bleeding, wailing in ache and looked half dead.

Khalid attempted a soft exit from his fishing boat, holding a rack sack in a calming manner, stepped down onto the shoreline with a thought of unfinished accomplishment lightning in his ego. He wanted to get closer to Samy and make sure he had done the job fully or attempt to get it done once and for all. In the back of Khalid's mind is Richard Caldwell waiting for a confirmation of the final ordeal which cost him a large lump of money. Khalid knew he had to do the job or risk being a possible target himself should Richard decide to go on that malevolent path. Khalid was reaching out for his rack sack while holding it with his left hand, the moment he inserted his right hand in it he fell down with a hit of a shot fired at his upper body.

Tony had been hidden behind a kiosk overshadowed by two very large palm trees, he had witnessed the whole scene and read between the lines. Tony waved at Marco

showing that they had to leave fast, in the same manner as he did,
and disappeared from the site as few people were running toward Khalid for his aid.

Daniel was left on his own bearing the ache of a malfunctioned cocktail dosed by his trainee. He would recover from it shortly after the agony of the spinning trip ceased effectively.

Marco sailed away to Seroza island minded that Samy had been shot and in need of treatment he pushed the trawler to its limits, the Sockeye 42 was twelve and a half meters long fishing boat, she was

a little rusty and a bit heavy to manoeuvre but capable of continued thrust.
Noah was so sick that he puked out onto the sea, worried about his father whether he would make it

or not.

-"Dad…" Noah baffled.

-"I'm good, son, it's not so bad. We'll make it, soon we'll be on land, I know someone who can help us." Samy claimed in grunts of pain.

-"Why dad? What did you do that made you act like a runaway? Aren't you getting old enough to be wiser now?" Asked Noah with a smile on his face.

-"Boy, I met this beautiful woman once, I knew she had the same interest in me as I had in her. I knew
I was married to your mother, but there was something about Jenny I could not stop looking at, she was a beautiful woman." Samy continued explaining.

-"We ended up talking, we simply clicked and eventually got too close to each other and… we were deep." Samy paused, looking saddened by the memories flashing his inner screen.

-"Is this why they want to kill you?" Noah asked.

-"No, Jenny fell off a hotel balcony in Spain but I had nothing to do with her death. I wasn't there at all. The man who was married to Jenny thinks I stole and killed her. He wants revenge." Samy confessed in a deep husky voice tone.

It didn't take long before reaching the shore on the north eastern side of Seroza island. Marco had contacted Samy's acquaintance from his little boat, who was already standing there on their arrival. They were driven to a secluded location. There were no authority agents, and the minute amount of habitants most likely were asleep or indoors. Samy got the treatment done, that hit was as life threatening as his brain tumour. He had a rest for

a day before flying out alone to Cape Verde where he lingered on the remaining days of his life time.
Marco had been a valuable resource as much as a great friend. He needed to get back before daylight. Marco

had discovered Elisa's contact through

Samy's accord and let her know that Noah was landing in London at a specific time. He had arranged the tickets for each and he was highly thanked by Noah and his father.

Noah had to remain for the rest of the night with the hospitality and company of Samy's acquaintance who would also take him to his flight for London bound early morning.

A mixed bag of emotions were residing in Noah's heart while he sat on the plane ready for take off, however he had a sense of urgency as much as it was a relief. He was still in paranoia, lacking nutrition and sleep, grasping so many events in such a short time. In contrast, the thought of Elisa made him feel calmer and brought him a shade of a smile.

At the same time in London Elisa was constantly checking her wrist watch or any other available display of time. She headed to the airport, and stood waiting anxiously at the arrival meeting point. Elisa spotted Noah's image walking out of the arrivals gate as she ran to him feeling relieved he was still

in one piece, as well as declaring a burst of

happiness in her shiny eyes just as she threw herself at him, they wrapped around each other's body reaffirming their bond. It seemed too distant
a feeling that only for a few days her heart ache
was nearly impossible to cope with.
Both were aware that by remaining in London they run a higher risk of being spotted or chased. Noah thought of the man he had never met, Richard, whether he would

continue his quest to kill his dad
and possibly himself, judging by the turn of the events. Noah had to consider that Daniel would eventually return to London and meet Victor, who would know the truth about the outcome, by then. Victor had to commit to a decision of his own, would he lie to Richard and disregard the true facts of his request, or would he be truthful knowing that himself

would be a continuous asset in chasing Samy?

After all Richard was nearly in his sixtieth year, he was also getting a tad too tired of the pain that
Samy and Jenny caused him. He could not have put more emphasis on that subject. He had attempted this in the past unsuccessfully. Perhaps time has come to let it go.

Noah owned a villa in southern Portugal where he could settle for a new challenge in life. Maria had moved there permanently, counting the days before her time. She had been enjoying gardening as a methodical trait for meditative purposes and a sense of well-being and emotional recovery from all recent activities and changes in her life. She was hopeful that her son, and his well wished girlfriend, would be able to live there. Elisa had been highly thoughtful towards her future mother-in-law, even though at a distance, regularly phoned Maria to check on her health's implications as well as the overall development of her new life in western Algarve, generally maintaining a caring and an impressive rapport with her boyfriend's mother.

Two months later, Noah and Elisa were in Greece for a couple of weeks of relaxation. They were happy, holding hands, slowly walking along a very colourful and busy market. A wonderful sense of holiday was declared on the way they walked. In the distance stood an onlooker in shades, he leant against a stall's pole who suddenly started walking

in the opposite direction.
Noah looked over his
shoulder gracefully.
Tony and cousin Noah hadn't
met while the situation
developed at Sky Village.
Eventually Noah called him
to thank him for his help and
effort and Noah promised to
pay him a visit sometime in
the near future should the
occasion rise accordingly.

It had been a chain reaction
of events and decisions
which led to Noah meeting

his dad. Had he not had the hit and run accident marking an end to football, had he moved to London and meet people who made introductions and insightful comments on how to achieve a wealthier income, had he not decided
to accept the assignment which led him to flight out of London to a different country in order to

accomplish it, he most certainly would have not

expected it to have
happened naturally.

No one knows what the
future holds ahead, based
upon that, any ulterior
purpose may not take place.
Whether there are risks
being taken or not a lot of it
is to do with one's decisions
and sometimes it arises from
the outer surroundings.
The progression of time will
have confirmation whether it
was worth it or not. Who's to
say that there aren't

worsening scenarios yet to be faced? Anyone thinks of reality with a different perspective, which is not the same as defining it.
There are no certainties which can make anyone really be assured of planning ahead of time.

From the starting point to the development and to the potential outcome the trajectory is full of surprises.

The End

The Sky Village Assignment

A Plot In Paradise

The Sky Village Assignment

Paulo J. Santos © 2021

Printed in Great Britain
by Amazon